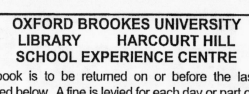

Liz Lewis

While Barnaby plays on the beach at Shell Bay, he spies a small dinghy drifting away!

Then Barnaby hears a terrified shout.
'Help - a strong current is taking us out!'

Barnaby phones without hesitation, the lifeboat man at the Coastguard Station.

'Two boys are in danger, out on the sea.
Send out the lifeboat - how long will it be?'

'Keep still and don't panic,'
Dad calls to the pair.
'Help is coming. Look - over there!'

They can hear a loud engine and see the white spray, as the powerful lifeboat zooms over the bay.

Into the lifeboat they lift Rick and Pete, and wrap them in blankets to keep in the heat.

Their parents are thrilled now they're safely on land. And they thank everyone and shake Barnaby's hand.

But Barnaby being a sensible bear, looks very stern and says to the pair:

'The sea is a dangerous place to play. There are very strong currents that sweep you away.'

'So tell all your friends to be careful too, for you owe your lives to the lifeboat crew.'